ROSIE BELLE

By
Martha Mann

To order additional copies of this book, contact:
Xlibris
844-714-8691
www.Xlibris.com
Orders@Xlibris.com

ISBN: 978-1-4415-3643-3 (sc)
ISBN: 978-1-4363-8318-9 (hc)

Print information available on the last page

Rev. date: 09/09/2024

To The Readers:

"ROSIE BELLE"
is an unusual pet.

Rosie loves to eat
vegetables, fruits,
seafood and roses!

Loving, beautiful,
talented and enchanting,
"ROSIE BELLE"
will charm you!

"Rosie Belle,

Aren't you swell!"

You are loud when you talk."

"White as a snowball,

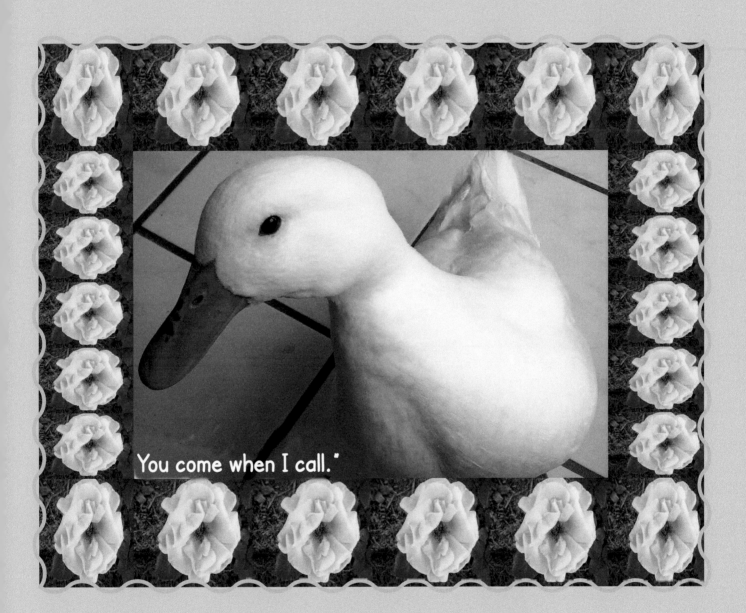

You come when I call."

"With your eyes so blue,

And your web feet, too.

Swimming in the pool,

"Running on the ground,

With the
pitter-patter sound."

"Flying in the air,

You have
talent to spare.

"Laying an egg almost every day,

Never meaning harm.'

"You make me laugh and grin,

Printed in the United States
by Baker & Taylor Publisher Services